Who

wants a cheap Rhinoceros?

by Shel Silverstein

50TH ANNIVERSARY EDITION

SIMON & SCHUSTER BOOKS FOR YOUNG READERS
New York London Toronto Sydney New Delhi

Revised and expanded edition of a book previously
published under the pseudonym Uncle Shelby

SIMON & SCHUSTER BOOKS FOR YOUNG READERS
An imprint of Simon & Schuster Children's Publishing Division
1230 Avenue of the Americas, New York, New York 10020
SIMON & SCHUSTER BOOKS FOR YOUNG READERS is a trademark of Simon & Schuster, Inc.
For information about special discounts for bulk purchases, please contact Simon & Schuster Special
Sales at 1-866-506-1949 or business@simonandschuster.com.
The Simon & Schuster Speakers Bureau can bring authors to your live event.
For more information or to book an event, contact the Simon & Schuster Speakers
Bureau at 1-866-248-3049 or visit our website at www.simonspeakers.com.
Book design by Kim Llewellyn
The text for this book is set in Bembo.
The illustrations for this book are rendered in pen and ink.
Manufactured in China
0918 SCP
10 9 8 7 6 5
The Library of Congress has catalogued a previous edition as follows:
Silverstein, Shel.
    Who wants a cheap rhinoceros?
    Summary: There are lots of things a rhino can do around one's house,
including eating bad report cards before one's parents see them, tiptoeing
downstairs for a midnight snack, and collecting extra allowance.
    1. Rhinoceros—Fiction. I. Title.
PZ7.S588Wh 2002 [E] 82-23945
ISBN 978-0-689-85113-1 (hc)
ISBN 978-1-4814-1593-4 (50th anniversary edition)

To Meg and Curt

Who wants a cheap rhinoceros?
I know of one for sale,
With floppy ears and cloppy feet,
And friendly waggy tail.
He's sweet and fat and huggable.
He's quiet as a mouse.
And there are lots of things that he
Can do around your house.

    For instance...

You can use him for a coat hanger.

He is a terrific back scratcher.

And he makes a very lovely lamp.

He will eat bad report cards
before your parents see them.

But he is not too great at opening doors.

He makes a good bloody ferocious pirate.

He can open soda cans for your uncle.

And on Sunday
you can read him
the comics.

He will be glad to turn a jump rope . . .

. . . if he gets his turn.

He's not too careful about
watching where he walks.

But he's very handy for collecting extra allowance from your father.

He makes an unsinkable battleship.

But he is not too interested in taking his bath.

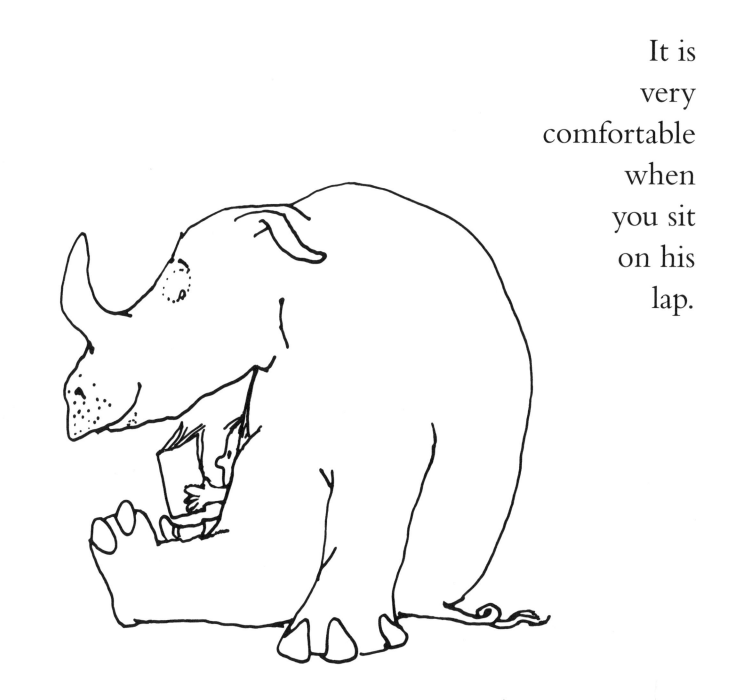

It is
very
comfortable
when
you sit
on his
lap.

but
not too
comfortable
when
he sits
on your
lap.

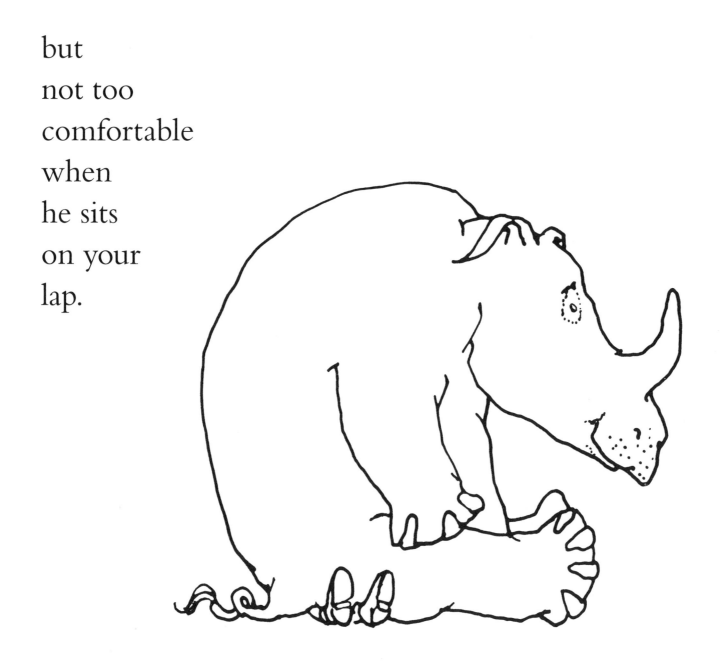

He's terrific at helping
your grandmother make donuts.

And he is great for not letting your mother hit you when you haven't really done anything bad.

He is very nice about crawling into bed
with you on cold winter nights,

and he is pretty good at
tiptoeing downstairs
for a midnight
snack.

And he'll gladly eat scraps from the table.

He is terrific at being Ben and Charlie,
two desperate crooks.

And he loves to surprise you.

He will be glad to help your aunt
knit a sweater.

Especially if it is for him.

He is careful about not leaving rhinoceros
tracks around the house.

He is fun to take care of
when he is sick.

And he is great for plowing your field if you are a farmer.

He is hard to build a house for.

But he is lots of fun
at the beach

because he is great at imitating a shark.

And he is easy to love.

He is good for yelling at.

He loves to play
hide and seek.

And on Halloween you can dress him up
like a girl—but he won't like it.

He is wonderful
for playing records
if you have
no record player.